Prairie Dogs Kiss and Lobsters Wave

· How Animals Say Hello ·

MARILYN SINGER

Illustrated by NORMAND CHARTIER

Henry Holt and Company · New York

To Easy, who loves to say hello
— M.S.

With a kiss for Matt and Rubia, and
a pet for Ginger, Shelby, Patches, and Bruiser
— N.C.

Introduction

When people meet each other, they shake hands, slap five, smile, salute, bow, embrace, say *Yo*. *Hello*. *How are you*? *Good morning*. *Good evening*. *What's up*? *What's new*? They may be happy to see each other. They may not care very much at all.

Strangers greet each other differently than people who know each other well. You wouldn't greet a new kid at school the same way you'd greet your best friend. You wouldn't say hello to your mother the same way you'd say hello to the president of the United States. Most greetings are friendly or polite. Some aren't. Some greetings show respect for a person's rank. Most probably don't.

The same is true of animals. Their greetings are as many and varied as the species themselves. You know how people greet each other. But what are animal greetings like? When animals meet their own kind, just what do they do?

Dogs Sniff

Dogs have an amazing sense of smell—maybe forty times better than people's. So it's no surprise that dogs use their noses to say hello.

When dogs and other members in the *canine*, or dog, family, such as wolves and coyotes, meet, they smell each other's faces and hindquarters. Sniffing can tell each dog whether the other one is a male or a female, whether it's a grown-up or a puppy, and whether it wants to mate or not.

If they're friendly, dogs welcome each other with wagging tails, upright or forward ears, bows, and happy barks. If they're not, they greet each other with drooping or stiff tails, flattened ears, bared teeth, and growls.

Like most other canines, dogs are social animals and like to travel in packs. Within a pack, whether it's large or small, each dog has a rank. Their body language when they greet tells which dog is dominant—has a higher rank—or if they're equals. A top dog will stand tall and straight and stare right at the other dog. Sometimes it will put its head or neck on the other dog's shoulder. An underdog will bow its head, lower its body, and look away. It may even lie down on its side or back. Equals don't threaten or act defenseless. Their greetings are brief and often lead to playing or to ignoring each other. Even though most pet dogs don't live in packs, when they meet other dogs, they act as if they do.

Dogs learn this body language when they're pups. Soon they become good at learning who's the boss and which other dogs to play with or stay away from. If you learn dogs' body language, you can figure out which dogs to play with or stay away from too.

Prairie Dogs Kiss

Out on the western American plains, groups of prairie dogs live together in big underground burrows called towns. Each town can have as many as fifteen prairie dogs living in it. Prairie dogs aren't dogs at all—they're squirrel-like rodents. And for them, as for many other animals, living in a group is good protection against enemies. Each group of prairie dogs always has a guard or two on duty. These guards give an alarm call when they see danger.

Prairie dogs are friendly to members of their town, but not to strangers. When two prairie dogs meet, they approach each other cautiously. If they are strangers, they try to bite each other. If they are relatives or neighbors, they kiss—with lips open and teeth bared. Sometimes it's a quick kiss; sometimes it's longer, with one prairie dog rolling over on its back while it's still kissing. After the kiss, the prairie dogs may huddle, groom, play, or go off to feed, sometimes with their bodies still pressed together.

You might like to greet your friends and relatives with a kiss too, but probably not all the time, and certainly not prairie-dog style.

Walruses Breathe

Walruses are big, noisy animals with long tusks. They live in big, noisy colonies on small, rocky islands, sand spits, or ice floes. Most of the year, males and females live in separate groups in different places. The members of each group sleep next to each other on land or ice and hunt together in the water for clams, crabs, worms, snails, and sometimes seals.

Sleeping and hunting in a group gives protection against the walruses' chief enemies, the killer whale and the polar bear. Like other animals that live in groups, walruses need to be able to recognize and greet their friends and neighbors to feel safe and comfortable. They also need to tell these neighbors who's boss.

When a walrus hauls itself out on land or ice, it displays its tusks to the neighboring walruses to show how dominant it is. A walrus of equal rank may display its tusks in return. A lower-ranking walrus will turn its back or duck its head. The walruses all seem to be saying, "I'm here to rest. And I'm claiming this spot. Now don't bother me."

In the water, however, walruses have a friendlier way to greet and identify each other. There, they touch noses and inhale each other's breath. This is called exchange breathing.

Walruses that enter the water to hunt in a group will all exchange breath. The noise, which sounds like horses' snorting, is so loud it can be heard on shore a hundred yards—a whole football field—away. Perhaps, like football players rousing each other for a big game, the walruses are showing their form of team spirit, pepping up each other for their big hunt.

Lobsters Wave

A wave is a friendly greeting. But not to a lobster.

Lobsters are crustaceans—animals that usually live in water and have hard outer coverings that they shed and regrow, as well as jointed legs, cutting or crushing jaws, and two sets of antennae. Like most crustaceans, lobsters live alone. They don't want other lobsters in their territory, and they don't have much reason to be friendly.

When one male lobster is approached by another lobster, it will smell the stranger by moving its antennae, and raise and open its big claws in a most unfriendly wave. If the stranger is a female, the male may close his claws and let her pass. If it's another male and he doesn't back off, the two may fight, grabbing and pinching with those same big claws. When two female lobsters meet, they also wave open claws and they too will fight if one does not retreat. Sometimes one lobster releases—purposely sheds—a claw in battle. Then the other lobster usually eats it. The lost claw will eventually grow back.

You might say that a lobster's hello is more like, "Get going. Good-bye!"

Giraffes Lick

Giraffes like to lick. They groom themselves by licking, and they groom each other by licking too. So it's no surprise that when members of a herd meet, they nuzzle and lick each other's body, head, mane, horns, or eyes. Usually one giraffe licks the other, but sometimes they both do it at the same time. A brand-new baby is welcomed into the herd by being licked and nuzzled too.

Unlike many other groups, giraffe herds are loose. Members come and go. This is because giraffes see well and don't rely on each other as much for protection as some other animals do. But even though their relationships may be casual, giraffes like a lot of physical contact. Besides licking and nuzzling, giraffes will sometimes rub their heads or legs against each other.

Rubbing those long necks is a kind of greeting too—but not a friendly one. Male giraffes rub their necks to show who's boss. The rubbing may lead to actual fighting—slapping necks together and jabbing horns—until one giraffe finally backs down. But after the fight, giraffes don't hold grudges. The same giraffes who were fighting one day may lick each other hello when they meet again.

Chimps Hug

The way people greet each other has a lot to do with how they feel about each other and how long they've been apart. The same is true of chimpanzees. Some chimp greetings are just a grunt and a quick glance. But others are loud and happy. When chimps who are good friends or family members meet after a long separation, they fling their arms around each other, hug, and kiss. They may also make eager grunts or screams. At other times, they may pat their companions, hold hands, bow, grin, or thump each other on the back. Males may chuck females or babies under the chin.

All of these greetings seem humanlike. But chimp greetings can also be very different from human greetings. A lower-ranking chimp greeting a dominant one may bob up and down rapidly or crouch low to the ground and make a series of panting grunts. Female chimps will sometimes show their rear ends to high-ranking males. This is a way of asking the males not to attack them.

When some chimps meet—for example, a mother and daughter who have been apart for just a short time—they immediately begin to groom each other, picking off bugs and bits of dead skin. Sometimes when a group of chimps that has been separated reunites, the greeting is excited and aggressive. Dominant chimps, usually males, hit or jump on lower-ranking ones. But afterward, these same chimps often hug, kiss, and groom one another. For people, greeting and talking often go together. For chimpanzees, it's greeting and grooming.

Bees Feel

If you were as busy as a bee, you'd be very busy indeed. Every day honeybees fly out of their hive to search for nectar and pollen. When they return with the food, each and every worker is greeted by the hive's guards. The guards sweep their antennae over the arrivals, examining them thoroughly. What are the guards looking for? The right smell.

Each honeybee colony has its own special odor, and each bee in the colony has the same smell. A bee's sense of smell is in the last eight

joints of its antennae. When a guard feels a worker with its antennae, it's checking to make sure the returning bee has the right odor, that it's really a member of that colony. Then the guard will let the worker come in.

What happens if a bee is not from that hive? It may be allowed in but offered less food until it acquires the colony odor. It may be driven from the hive. Or it may be killed. Some young and confused bees who fly into the wrong hive are actually picked up by the guards and dumped somewhere away from the hive. With luck, those intruders will find their own hive, where the guards' greetings will be a lot less rough.

Elephants Touch

A trunk is a handy thing. An elephant uses it to breathe, to trumpet, to pick up and carry things, to nudge naughty babies, and also to greet other elephants.

Elephants live in large family groups made up of related females and their children. Males live alone, or sometimes in all-male groups. Greeting ceremonies are very important to the family groups, because they help the members stay friendly and close. When elephants meet, they explore each other with their trunks, touching faces, reaching into mouths, and sniffing cheeks and bodies. They entwine their trunks as well, in an elephant version of a kiss.

Elephants also greet by clicking their tusks together, flapping their ears, spinning and turning, urinating and defecating, trumpeting and rumbling. A greeting rumble is low and throaty. Elephants make other rumbles too, which people can feel but not hear. These sounds carry as far as six miles and are used by elephants to stay in contact, to coordinate movements, and to find mates.

From their low rumbles and loud greetings, it's easy to see that elephants like to keep in touch.

Bears Circle

Unless you're asking for a fight, you're not likely to walk around and around someone when you meet him or her. But then, you're not a bear.

Bears greet by circling one another, sniffing and watching as they do to see who's bigger and stronger and to find out whether to attack, retreat, or get along. A bear about to attack will lower its head, flatten its ears, and stare at its opponent. It may growl or make a threatening open-mouthed charge. A smaller bear will usually run from a large one. A bear of equal or larger size may threaten back or fight. Or the bears may decide to be friends. Friendly bears keep their heads low and don't stare. Then, one of them may touch the other's nose, sit down, and clasp its jaws or chew its neck slowly and gently. This sort of biting may lead to playful pushing and wrestling.

You probably wouldn't enjoy this kind of greeting. But then, you're not a bear.

Zebras Chew

Once upon a time, when people shook hands they did it to show they weren't carrying weapons. Zebras don't shake hands. They have a different way to show they don't intend to fight.

Many zebra herds are made up of several females, or mares, and one male, or stallion, who's the leader. When certain types of zebra stallions from different herds meet, they first sniff noses. Then, standing opposite each other or side by side, they make a special "greeting face"—they bend their ears forward, pull back their lips, and chew. By chewing or biting the air, zebras show they won't chew or bite each other.

If the stallions are equals, they'll continue the greeting ceremony by moving head to tail, pushing their heads against each other's flanks and rubbing up and down. Then they'll sniff noses again and spring apart in a farewell jump. Zebras who live in all-male groups perform the same ceremony, but not necessarily in the same order. At the end of the greeting, one zebra will often put his head on the other's back. Mares and stallions will greet this way too. Mares greeting other mares generally just sniff noses, call out, and prance a little.

Zebra greetings may be longer and more complicated than some other animal greetings, but they work—for zebras.

Luminous Fish Glow

Have you ever communicated with someone by using a flashlight, flicking it on and off to say, "Hello, here I am"? Luminous fish do something like that all the time.

Luminous fish create their own light, using chemicals or chemical-producing bacteria in their bodies. There are many kinds of these fish. Each has its own pattern, order, and color of light signals, and each can recognize its own species from these signals.

One type of luminous fish—the flashlight fish—has greenish lights

on its face that glow like car headlights. These headlights help the fish navigate through dark water, see and catch prey, and defend its territory. When another fish swims near its home, the female flashlight fish will turn off its lights, swim close to the other fish, and suddenly turn on its lights in a startling flash. To escape an enemy, a flashlight fish will zigzag away, blinking its lights on and off rapidly to confuse the predator. To greet a friend or mate, a flashlight fish will keep still and blink its lights quickly, straight at the other fish.

You might claim that you glow when you meet a good friend. But a flashlight fish really does.

Geese Stretch

When a goose sticks out its long neck, it might be acting brave, it might be picking a fight, or it might be saying, "Nice to see you again." How do you know what a goose is communicating? Even more important, how does another goose? The answer is in the angle.

A goose greeting a companion will stretch out its neck and hold it at an angle, curving it past its partner. At the same time, it will cackle. The more excited the goose is to see its mate or relative or friend, the more it will slant its head and neck and the louder and faster it will call.

Geese usually live in pairs or family groups. They spend a lot of time defending each other. A goose that is acting brave or threatening another goose will stretch its neck and head straight forward with no slant and stare right at the enemy, often hissing as it does. If the goose successfully chases away the enemy, it will return to its mate and give a special triumph greeting, stretching out its neck, holding its head at an angle just above the ground, and gabbling loudly at its partner's ear. Entire geese families perform a type of triumph greeting too, after they've chased away another group of geese.

The triumph greeting ceremony is sort of a goose's version of a high five—a very loud version indeed.

Whales Whistle

Every person who can write has a signature—a special, individual way of signing his or her name. Dolphins also have a type of signature—a signature whistle. A dolphin will use that whistle to identify itself and say hello when it meets another dolphin, as well as to show how it's feeling. Scientists have learned that dolphins can recognize not only their friends and relatives by their whistles, but their emotional states by these sounds as well.

Dolphins are actually whales. Toothed whales, to be exact. Toothed whales tend to be very sociable, living and traveling in family groups called pods. Besides using whistles to keep in contact, different types of whales in different pods will greet and communicate with each other through chirps, grunts, cries, and clicks. Some of these sounds are too high for people to hear. Because sound travels well in water, it makes sense that whales use sound to communicate.

Whales often try to communicate with people as well as with other whales. We don't yet understand much of what they're saying to us or to each other, but we do know that they like to talk. A lot.

Much thanks for their literary and scientific help to Steve Aronson,
Kathy Darling, Dr. Sue Hills, Dr. Bryn Mader, Tom Probst, Paul
Sieswerda, Ed Spevack, excellent fact checker Roland Smith, my
wonderful editor Simone Kaplan, and the staff at Henry Holt.

Henry Holt and Company, Inc.
Publishers since 1866
115 West 18th Street
New York, New York 10011

Published in Canada by Fitzhenry & Whiteside Ltd., 195 Allstate Parkway, Markham, Ontario L3R 4T8.
Library of Congress Cataloging-in-Publication Data
Singer, Marilyn. Prairie dogs kiss and lobsters wave: how animals say hello / Marilyn Singer;
illustrated by Normand Chartier.
1. Animal communication. 2. Social behavior in animals. I. Chartier, Normand. II. Title.
QL776.S59 1996 591.59—dc20   96-44255
ISBN 0-8050-3703-9 / First Edition—1998
Printed in the United States of America on acid-free paper. ∞
1 3 5 7 9 10 8 6 4 2